I0531002

If You Give a Girl a Diamond

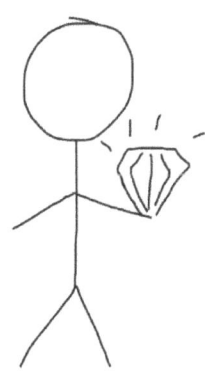

ISBN: 978-0-578-94306-0

Text and Illustrations Copyright © 2021 by Jason Woodcock

All rights reserved.

This book is dedicated to my wife and daughter who endure my dry sense of humor every day. Thank you.

If you ask a girl to marry you, she's going to want a diamond. And, if you give a girl a diamond, she'll want to plan a wedding. If she's going to plan a wedding, she will need a dress.

She'll ask you to take her dress shopping. On the way to the dress store, she'll see a real estate office. She'll stop to look at the listings in the window. Looking at the listings will remind her that you don't yet live together, so she picks a place and you move in together.

Moving in together, she'll realize there is too much stuff. She'll ask you to put your things on the lawn for a tag sale. While carrying things out to the lawn she'll notice other tag sales of men's belongings, which makes her think of shopping. She'll ask you to take her to the mall.

Driving through the mall parking lot, she'll see a minivan. Seeing a minivan makes her think of children. She'll ask to have a baby.

After shopping for children's clothes, you drive home to have a baby. On the way home you'll drive by a cat shelter.

She'll ask you to stop. She'll rush in to look at all the cats, and, after several hours, will bring home the first cat she saw. Hearing the cat meow in the car will make her think of her childhood.

Thinking of her childhood, she'll remember the glorious wedding that she had planned – the gown, the reception, the cake.

Thinking of the wedding, she'll look down at her hand. When she looks down at her hand, she'll think of a diamond.

And, chances are, if she's thinking about a diamond, you'll have to ask the girl to marry you.

The End

www.ingramcontent.com/pod-product-compliance
Lightning Source LLC
Chambersburg PA
CBHW080813120626
46556CB00009B/3312